Sweet Dreams!

Susan Poca-Koch

11/11/16

Get Out of My Head

of My Head

I Should Go to Bed

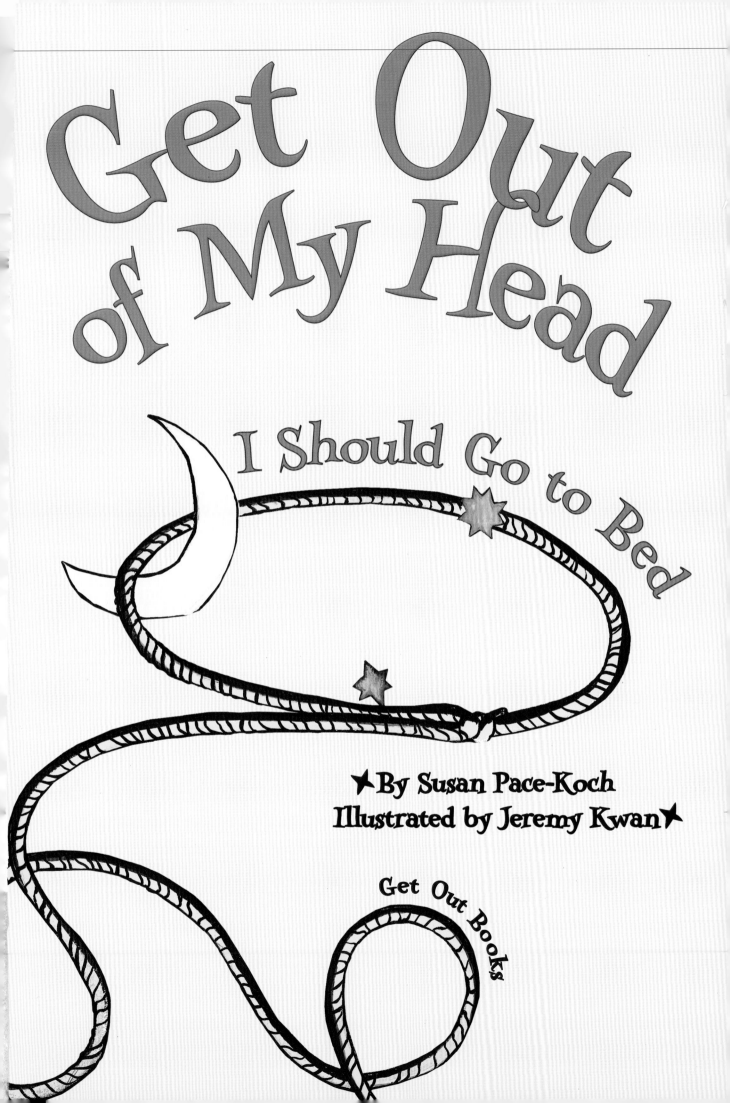

★By Susan Pace-Koch
Illustrated by Jeremy Kwan★

Get Out Books

To Allison and Christopher for the wonderful memories of reading, listening and sharing stories together. To Bill for his unending support and encouragement.—SPK

For mom, dad, and Oma because you've never stopped showing how much you care.—JK

Text © 2011 Susan Pace-Koch
Illustration © 2011 Jeremy Kwan

Printed and bound in China by Regent Publishing Services Limited
Printed January, 2011 in China

Book design and computer production by Patty Arnold, *Menagerie Design & Publishing*
www.menageriedesign.net

GET OUT BOOKS

2020 Bonifacio Street, Concord, California, 94520-2208
www.getoutbooks.com
ISBN 978-0-9829608-0-6

Good Day Poem

A good day has come to an end
    A night's sleep is around the bend

Heavy tho' my eyes may be
    Too many thoughts for me to see

How can I close my eyes and rest
    Sleep now is my only quest

So go away things, right now I mean
    I'm ready now for my goodnight dreams

Horse and Saddle

Longhorn Cattle

Get out of my head

I should go to bed !

Castles and Kings

Sailboats with Wings

Give me some peace

I just need some sleep

Witches and Wizards

Dinosaurs and Lizards

Let me alone

To bed in my room

Mansions and Caves

Spooky dark Graves

I'm feeling weary

My eyes are so bleary

Sweet Dreams

Ships and Docks

Huge building Blocks

No more play

I'm starting to sway

Puppies and Kittens

Finding lost Mittens

Let's count sheep

Like Little Bo Peep

Giants and Frogs

Pirates and Dogs

I think I need rest

No treasure chest

Duckies and Dragons

Little red Wagons

I'm all wound up

I want to wind down

Bears and Balloons

Bikes and Baboons

My eyes are so heavy

I just need my teddy

Dolphins and Whales

Kid's Fairy Tales

Get out of my head

I should go to bed!

Just close my eyes now . . .

Good dreams to follow . . .

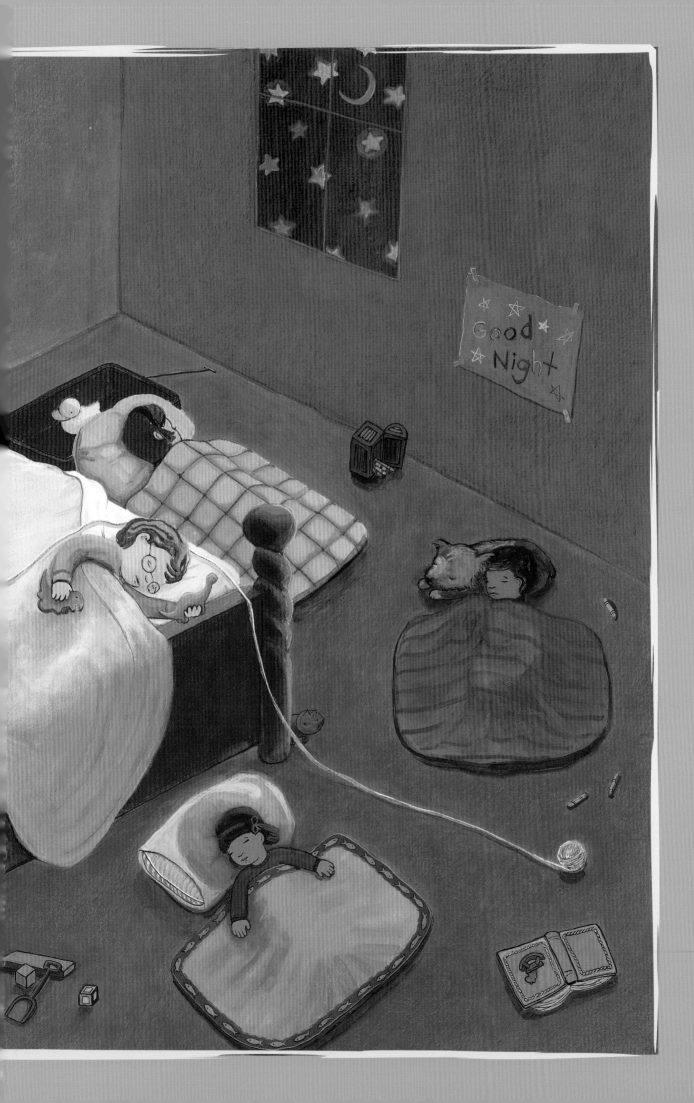

Good Night Poem

Now as I lay down to sleep

Nice and quiet, not a peep

Keep me safe through the night

Wake me in the morning light